THE GOLLYWHOPPER EGG

Weekly Reader Children's Book Club presents

THE GOLLYWHOPPER EGG

Anne Rockwell

Ready-to-Read

MACMILLAN PUBLISHING CO., INC.

New York

Macmillan Publishing Co., Inc., 866 Third Avenue, New York, N.Y. 10022
Collier-Macmillan Canada Ltd.
Library of Congress catalog card number: 73-6042
Printed in the United States of America

2 3 4 5 6 7 8 9 10

Library of Congress Cataloging in Publication Data

Rockwell, Anne F
The gollywhopper egg.
(A Ready-to-read book)
I. Title.
PZ7.R5943Go [E] 73-6042 ISBN 0-02-777470-8

Weekly Reader Children's Book Club Edition

for Hannah, Elizabeth and Oliver

CHAPTER ONE

Timothy Todd was a peddler.
He peddled buttons, bottles,
and bandannas,
molasses and needles and nails.

He peddled hoes and hatchets
and hammers,
saws and scissors and tea.

He peddled pots and pans and pins,
and calico cloth and castor oil.

He peddled things from the city
to farmers in the country.
They paid him with
corn and pigs, bacon and beans,
dollars and cents.

One day Timothy Todd
bought a coconut from a sailor.

He tried to peddle it.

But no one had ever seen a coconut.

No one had ever eaten one.

No one wanted to buy one.

"It has sweet milk,"
said Timothy Todd.
"So does our cow," a farmer said.
"It has good white meat,"
said Timothy Todd.
"So do my chickens,"
said the farmer's wife.

Timothy Todd walked
down the road.
"No one wants my sweet coconut,"
he said.
"I can peddle buttons and bottles
and bandannas.
I can peddle molasses and needles
and pins.
But I cannot peddle my coconut.
I will have to think."

CHAPTER TWO

Timothy Todd came
to Farmer Foote's house.

He peddled four buttons
for two pounds of beans.
He peddled one bottle for ten cents.
He peddled five bandannas
for five cents each.
He peddled some sweet molasses,
a needle, and one hundred nails
for one fat pig.
"Now," said Timothy Todd
to Farmer Foote,
"I have something good.
I have something good
just for you."

MOLASSES
NAILS

He took the coconut out of his pack.
"What do you think this is?" he said.
"Shucks," said Farmer Foote,
"I don't know.
I never saw one before."

"I'll tell you a secret,"
said Timothy Todd.
"This is a gollywhopper egg."
"Gollywhopper egg?"
said Farmer Foote.
"What is a gollywhopper?"

CHAPTER THREE

"Oh, a gollywhopper is
a very good bird,"
said Timothy Todd.

"A gollywhopper can hoe a field,
hammer a nail, or thread a needle.
A gollywhopper can bake beans
and wash pots and pans.
A gollywhopper is as big as a cow,
as strong as a mule,
and as fast as a horse.
Oh, a gollywhopper
is a very good bird to have."

Farmer Foote looked at the coconut.
"You may buy this gollywhopper egg,"
said Timothy Todd.
"I saved it just for you."

"I'll bet a gollywhopper gets
as hungry as a pig,"
said Farmer Foote.
"And I already have
five fat pigs to feed.
That is enough for me.
No, thank you,
no gollywhopper eggs for me!"

"Shucks," said the peddler,
"gollywhoppers get hungry.
That is true.
But gollywhoppers can eat clouds
and rainbows, and even air.

They also like beans and bacon,
corn and molasses and tea.
But gollywhoppers
will even eat words!"
"Words?" said Farmer Foote.
"Oh, yes," said Timothy Todd.
"If you just say
cookies and candy, beans and bacon,
meat and molasses and milk,
a gollywhopper
isn't hungry anymore.
Oh, yes, gollywhoppers
are very good at eating words."

Farmer Foote looked at the coconut.
"In summer," said Timothy Todd,
"when it is hot,
a gollywhopper waves its wings.
Then the air is cool
for a hundred miles.

In winter, when it is cold,
one gollywhopper feather is warmer
than ten wool blankets
and a suit of long underwear.

You can ride a gollywhopper
all the way to town.

When you are lonesome,
a gollywhopper can sing
a sweet song.
But when you are sad,
a gollywhopper can stand
on his head
and make you laugh.
And when bears and bobcats
bother you,
your gollywhopper will screech
and scream and squawk
and scare them all away.

Oh, yes," said Timothy Todd,
"a gollywhopper is
a very good bird to have."

"Yes," said Farmer Foote,
"I think you are right.
I think a gollywhopper would be
a very good bird for me to have.
I will buy the gollywhopper egg!"

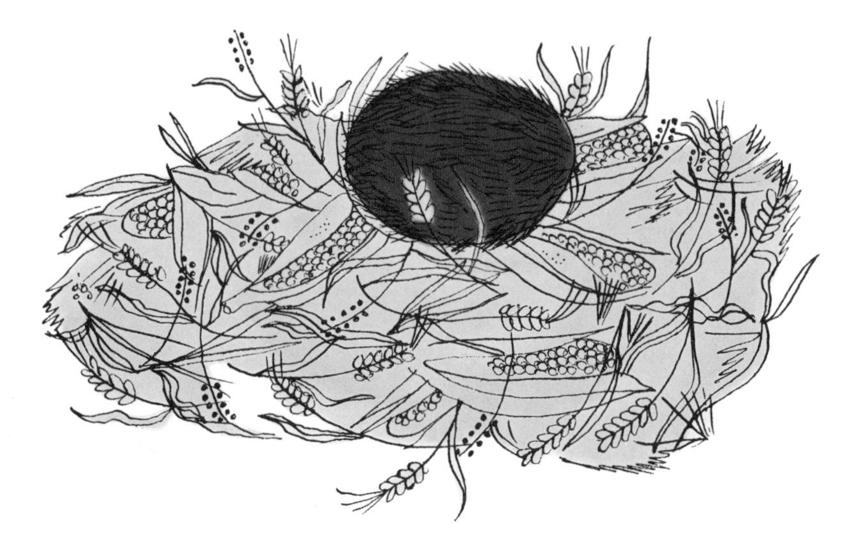

CHAPTER FOUR

Farmer Foote made
a nice warm nest
for his gollywhopper egg.
He made the nest of corn and hay.

He put a warm wool blanket
on the gollywhopper egg.
But the gollywhopper egg
did not hatch.

Farmer Foote listened
to the gollywhopper egg.
He wanted to hear the
"peck, peck peck"
of a little gollywhopper
hatching out.
But he could not hear a
"peck, peck peck."

"I will sit my chicken
on the gollywhopper egg,"
said Farmer Foote.
And the chicken sat for two weeks.

But the gollywhopper egg
did not hatch.

"I will sit my goose
on the gollywhopper egg,"
said Farmer Foote.
And the goose sat for two weeks.

But the gollywhopper egg
did not hatch.

"I will sit my pig
on the gollywhopper egg,"
said Farmer Foote.
But the pig would not sit.

"Then I will have to sit myself,"
said Farmer Foote.
And he sat on the gollywhopper egg
for two days.

He sang a song
while he sat on
the gollywhopper egg.
"Come out,
come out,
my gollywhopper.
For you are meant for me.
Oh, my gollywhopper,
how good you'll be to me."
He listened to hear a
"peck, peck peck."
But he did not hear any
"peck, peck peck."

The Gollywhopper egg
did not hatch.

Farmer Foote was angry.
Farmer Foote was so angry
he jumped up and down
and began to cry.

"Shucks!" he said.
"My chicken has sat.
My goose has sat.
My pig will not sit.
And I have sat.
And I have sung.
But my gollywhopper egg
will not hatch!
And a gollywhopper would be
such a good bird for me to have!"
And Farmer Foote was so angry
he kicked the gollywhopper egg.

He kicked it right out of the nest,
out of the door,
across the yard,
and into the field.

A little wild turkey
was sleeping in the field.
The coconut woke it up.

"Gobble, gobble, gobble!"
said the little wild turkey,
and ran out of the field,
into the woods,
and far away.

When Farmer Foote saw the
little wild turkey run away
he began to cry harder than ever.
"Oh, shucks!" he said.
"My gollywhopper egg hatched and
my little gollywhopper ran away!
Oh, and when it grew big,
it would have been
such a good bird for me to have!"

STORE
CORN

CHAPTER FIVE

Timothy Todd came peddling again.
Farmer Foote said,
"My gollywhopper egg hatched
and my little gollywhopper ran away.
Please, may I buy another?

My chicken will sit.
My goose will sit.
My pig will not sit.
But I will sit,
and sit,
and sing.
Please, may I buy
another gollywhopper egg?"

But Timothy Todd had no
gollywhopper eggs in his bag.

Not that month,
not the next month.

He never had a
gollywhopper egg again.

CHINA
TEA